Mythics

Seth Masek

Copyright © 2018 Seth Masek

All rights reserved. No part of this work may be reproduced, or stored in a retrieval system, or transmitted in any form or by any means, electronic, mechanical, photocopying, recording, or otherwise without written permission of the author.

2nd Edition
ISBN: 978-0999871249

Table of Contents

A Ballad to the Stars 11

Alone Again 13

In My Mind 14

Lexicon 16

And Now the Words Are Found 18

She Stands at the Threshold 20

Deep Inside Her Kiss 22

I Cannot Compete with Madness 23

Phoenix Cry 24

Work of She 26

Today I Found 28

I Swear 29

Glass in My Hands 31

My Lover 33

This World Needs Your Smile 35

Twilight 37

Her Kiss 38

Meet 39

Melting 40

Do I Keep Up? 42

Not Alone	44
Waking Up	45
She is Mine	47
Into the Deep	48
I Wish	49
Aimless Ashes	50
Magic Place	51
Magnets	53
Happy Song	55
My Best-Kept Secret	56
Her Eyes, Her Eyes	57
Between	58
She's Burning	60
Day was Long	61
New Song	62
You Make Me Special	64
Look at the Way	65
Heavens and Stars	67
Voracity	69
Save Some Time for Me	71
I Want	72
Our Dimensions	73
Birdsong	74

Wonderful Thing	75
Tonight	79
Together	81
So the Question Is	82
Room at My Side	84
Let's Take a Walk	86
I Need	87
Woke Up to You Talking	88
My Fire	90
Unbearable	91
Run to a Place	92
My Duty	93
Little Light	94
Bring Me Down	95
Winter-Born	97
Something New	98
Far Come	99
Is It Easier to Love Me?	100
Learned	101
Take the Time to Write It Down	103
She	104
What Happy Makes	105
Moments	107

Cheer	108
Thankful	110
Waking Up the Pen	111
Our Castle	113
Red Stone	117
MMXVI	119
I Felt You Yesterday	121
What I Write	122
I Hope You Know	123
What I Want Is Not Mine	124
My Little Lady	125
When It's Your Time	127
My Song	128
Sweet Verse	129
Count	131
Be My Burden	133
My Love	135
Such as I Have	138
What I Feel	139
Ropes	141
Your Words	142
For You Are Good	144
We Wander	145

Flower	146
Need	148
We Owe Each Other Nothing	149
Complements	150
Vision	152
My Eyes Be Blind	153
Providence	155
I Think of Things	156
Poet Out of Me	157
Can You Tell Me?	158
A Place	160
Surviving Charades	161
Today	163
My Life for Yours	164
What You Make	166
Oh My	167
Sit with Me	169
Mythics	173
What You Give	178
Mystery	179
Into a Space You Crept	180
More	182
Ode to a Phoenix	183

A Song for You 184

I Love Your Crazy 186

Don't Be to Me a Memory 188

Give Me Your Best 189

My Phoenix 191

My End 192

Mansion 194

Proud 197

Say It Again 199

A Poem for You 201

In Sickness and in Health 202

The Great Divide 203

Mutiny 205

Clarity 207

Time Set Aside 208

She Took My Pen 210

Lover 212

To the fiery ones, who by their madness drive us

A Ballad to the Stars

A billion stars, they fill the sky
But only one did catch my eye
I saw it shining bright one night
And focused in with all my might

A ballad to a billion stars
To make just one star see
A ballad to a billion stars
To make one fall for me

A light so brilliant but so far
How could I capture this, my star?
I invoked my only gift
And timeless words opened a rift

A message sent to outer space
I felt my little star's heart race
Her heat exceeded by her light
A shooting star born in the night

A ballad to a billion stars
To make just one star see
A ballad to a billion stars
To make one fall for me

This burning star toward my hands fell
A prized star from Orion's Belt
The red-hot flames that form her core
I hope one day I will explore

Alone Again

Alone again
In the dark
It's my favorite place to be

Alone again
Out of luck
It is my destiny

There is nowhere to retreat
Nothing I see is concrete
Why can't you and I meet?

Alone again
In my room
I can't sit still but cannot move

Alone again
Phasing out
My body twists and turns for you

There is nowhere to retreat
Nothing I see is concrete
Why can't you and I meet?

In My Mind

In my mind is another kind of time

In another kind of place with another kind of rhyme

There's nothing left to say; there's nothing left to learn

There's nothing but the future, and the future is our turn

Come and stay if only for a day

We're a different kind of something, and there's nothing else to say

Come and stay if only for a while

You're the sweetest kind of sweet, my little honey child

There you stand at the entrance to my hall

With a pencil in your hand and the writing on the wall

Listen to me, baby, let me sweep you off your feet

Let me fill you with my passion, let me move you with the beat

Come and stay; I only want to play

We're a different kind of something, and there's nothing else to say

Come and stay if only for a while

You're the sweetest kind of sweet, my little honey child

Would you sing it softly if I gave to you a song?

Would you take a side road with me if a million miles long?

Will I last for you a lifetime? Will we spoil in the sun?

Will we ever find the meaning, if we're only having fun?

Come and stay, I don't care the price I'll pay

We're a different kind of something, and there's nothing else to say

Come and stay if only for a while

You're the sweetest kind of sweet, my little honey child

Lexicon

Many poets filled their pages
Many sages spilled their souls
Their well is pure and won't run empty
Never have I reached that goal

You are perched so high above me
Looking down at what you've rent
As many men may pay for pleasure
All my wealth on you is spent

Why can't I have my lover?
Why must you make me start over?
I have no language but your song
You have become my lexicon

I am just a simple thinker
I cannot compel the mass
Trust that to which your soul may tether
Will you force out all the rest?

I will find the center in you
I'll espouse what you believe
Do you believe I'll elevate you?
Will you grant me a reprieve?

Why can't I have my lover?
Why must you make me start over?
I have no language but your song
You have become my lexicon

The type upon my fingers rest
Charting every thought I make
I will suffer through eternity
If at the end, you're mine to take

Can you see creation in me?
Can you tame the lion's roar?
No longer bound by fate's deterrence
Making love forevermore

Why can't I have my lover?
Why must you make me start over?
I have no language but your song
You have become my lexicon

And Now the Words Are Found

And now the words are found
From pools of vision, surround me
Her love for me abounding
In me, deeply

Fell victim to her praises
As Lazarus, she raises me
Her love for me astounding
In me, deeply

And now the words are found
I wear her passion like a crown
Lifted is the shroud
That covered me

And now the words are found
I fear no longer I will drown
Drawn out of the crowd
That smothered me

Soft you now, my orison
My every dream you send me
Her love for me resounding
In me, deeply

Weary souls igniting
Studying, delighting me
Her love for me compounding
In me, deeply

And now the words are found
I wear her passion like a crown
Lifted is the shroud
That covered me

And now the words are found
I fear no longer I will drown
Drawn out of the crowd
That smothered me

She Stands at the Threshold

She stands at the threshold
And I shut the door
She questions my actions
It's her I adore

She tells me she wants me
I echo her will
All these transactions
The pain worth the pill

She makes my mind wander
The visions delight
Despite warring factions
She is worth the fight

She takes time to meet me
I meet her halfway
Now that we have traction
We are here to stay

She's holding up Atlas
And though I may shrug
An endless attraction
I love her warm hugs

She makes love an object
That I must pursue
Gone from me inaction
I know our love true

Deep Inside Her Kiss

Deep inside her kiss
I felt all that I have missed
Life and love atop this list
Deep inside her kiss

Deep inside her kiss
A moment of imperfect bliss
She's made this poor man rich
Deep inside her kiss

Deep inside her kiss
In my life comes a new twist
For her lips, I'd bear all risks
Deep inside her kiss

I Cannot Compete with Madness

I cannot compete with madness
I cannot deliver rest
If you do not believe me
I cannot give my best

I cannot make sadness merry
I cannot mend broken hearts
If you are not to go with me
Then let it go before it starts

I cannot forgive the offense
I cannot the sleeping wake
If you are not to receive me
You will watch me crack and break

I cannot complete this love song
I cannot my eyes define
If you are not to deceive me
I'll find a way to walk the line

Phoenix Cry

Stand I as we, edge of forked path

Cannot step too quickly

The first road straight, trees well-groomed

Easy to walk, nowhere to roam

My heart calls to that path not forged

Just the vision steals my breath

What holds fate for me?

Am I prepared for that journey?

Do I need thick soles to walk that pavement?

Or a sharp knife to defend from wild?

Will I roam life's road alone?

I can't be protected from afar

I want a partner on this road

To see light when it's dark, to warm my soul when it's cold

Do not mistake my smiles for strength

I see the stars but do not live among

My world is fragile, stained as glass

Often times, I turn to ash

Will you be there to keep me calm?

Ease these fears?

Will you set me free?

Wipe these tears

Two roads, two worlds

Gravity pulls

Time can no longer stand still

Defend I must, but which?

Which yield first? Soles or souls?

Work of She

She's a work of art
I'm so convinced
She makes me sweat to pay the rent

She's a canvas clean
I'll fill her up
She's water pure that my heart pumps

She's a running stream
In which I fish
She is my dream, my one true wish

Does she know what she has made?
Does she know who she has saved?
Will she keep what she has found?
Will she run the ship aground?

She's a pristine pearl
From deep blue sea
She shines her crystals mystically

She's a prism bright
I'm so impressed
Her colors shine when she's undressed

She's a locket tight

Opened to me

Into her depth I've gained entry

Does she know what she has made?

Does she know who she has saved?

Will she keep what she has found?

Will she run the ship aground?

Today I Found

Today I found another way
A way to make an old man change
By a love so new and strange

Before the sun goes down today
This girl is going to know my name

Shadows of the past, I be
Be a path to set me free
Bring the key unto my cage

Before the sun goes down today
This girl is going to know my name

Swear it by your name
For her jewels, I'll pay the wage

Echoes through the canyon wall
Hearts poured like a waterfall
In the twilight, hear her call
Hand in hand, no fear at all

I Swear

I swear I hear the music
When I close my eyes
I swear I hear the music
Each note makes me high

I swear I feel the melody
When I start to dream
I swear I feel the melody
Smooth and calm and clean

Do you know how you make it real?
Make me hunger, make me feel
Do you know how you make it last?
Make me stronger, make me fast

I swear I knew the chamber
Where I hid away
I swear I knew the chamber
Where my heart was safe

I swear I know the reason
That I let you in
I swear I know the reason
How this did begin

Do you know how you make it real?
Make me hunger, make me feel
Do you know how you make it last?
Make me stronger, make me fast

I'm coming out for you
Never leaving you
I'm coming out for you
Take me home tonight

Glass in My Hands

Delicate was she in my hands
A precious vase from foreign land
Her eyes could melt the glassy sand
Make a window to the soul of man

All the earth was hers to wander
Her moves like the clouds to ponder
For her hand could none be fonder
Forgiving those who have wronged her

This past has passed; it has broken like glass
The currency of time is consumed so fast
This past has passed; now my hands cradle the glass
Love with passion is not destined to last

Soft her skin draped across my arms
Sheltered me from fear and harm
As the sun made a cold heart warm
Her beauty took so many forms

Truth a lesson learned painfully
Pursued her love I dutifully
Broken hearts chased for her wistfully
Eyes now see the world dystopically

This past has passed; it has broken like glass
The currency of time is consumed so fast
This past has passed; now my hands cradle the glass
Love with passion is not destined to last

My Lover

My lover, she's the servant

That makes the inside clean

My lover, she's the story

That we hope never ends

My lover, she's the goodness

That makes the poor man weep

My lover, she's the dagger

That makes the old-world bleed

My lover, she is lovely

My lover, she is whole

My lover, she is perfect

My lover, she's the wind

My lover, she's the dreamer

That makes the children dream

My lover, she's the traveler

That makes explorers send

My lover, she's the donor

That makes the rich man give

My lover, she's the savior

That makes the sick man live

My lover, she is lovely

My lover, she is whole

My lover, she is perfect

My lover, she's the wind

This World Needs Your Smile

I'll be happy either way
If you go or if you stay
But hear it clearly when I say
This world needs your smile

There are days that never end
In moments all I see is sin
Think I'm never going to win
This world needs your smile

Atlas shrugs, and Atlas sighs
Our headline news just falling skies
Some accept, and some ask why
This world needs your smile

Your smile is the light
Lights up a room and then takes flight
Our troubles slip and slide away
Your smile the light of each new day

Take these little verses
Now you know that it will nurse us
Those bright eyes do assure us
This world needs your smile

All our broken pieces
Jagged scars dwell just beneath us
Happiness trapped in the creases
This world needs your smile

Certainly, we see clearly
If we want to live life freely
Hold it tight, and love it dearly
This world needs your smile

Your smile is the light
Lights up a room and then takes flight
Our troubles slip and slide away
Your smile the light of each new day

Twilight

This kiss you gave my lips tonight
Will last with me for my whole life
Yielding not to Aeon's spite
Our love began in the twilight

Banded specters, black and white
Terrors dancing in moonlight
When you leave I lose my sight
My way is lit by the twilight

Wings of gold to air take flight
Enchanted feathers of a sprite
Fearing neither depth nor height
A fantasy in the twilight

Kisses born on a cold night
Orphaned in the warm daylight
Mischief managed to delight
Hand in hand in the twilight

Her Kiss

I should have known from the taste of her kiss
Her lips, a scarlet kris
I should have known from the feel of her hands
Her skin, the rolling sand

I should have known, I didn't see
How much inside of me was she
I should have known, but I didn't sense
How my heart she complements

I should have known from the way she smiled
Her eyes, free and wild
I should have known from the cut of her cloth
Her blaze, flowing rock

I should have known, but I didn't conceive
How made she my mind to believe
I should have known, but I didn't realize
How set she my feet in the skies

Meet

Every time we meet, a treat
We march to the drumbeat, hearts beat
Walking a new street, complete
Vow to never repeat, a feat

We have become what we were not
Survive the love, it's all we've got
We are to each our hemispheres
Two magnets drawn by hopes and fears

Every time we kiss, such bliss
We forget what we missed, a mist
Now our hearts insist, persist
Sworn never to resist, this kiss

We have become what we were not
Survive the love, it's all we've got
We are to each our hemispheres
Two magnets drawn by hopes and fears

Melting

Our minds will wax together while our bodies sway and rock

Just because I'm underwater doesn't mean that I can't talk

She's going to tell me what she wants; I'm going to give her what she needs

I'm going to make her cry my name into the air until it bleeds

One look, one touch, and she's melting fast for me

Her kisses set my soul ablaze, as she slides down onto her knees

My fingers clutch her wild hair, she sets the beast inside me free

Her hungry eyes unlock the cage and then receives me openly

My little lady takes the stage and triggers each and every nerve

I've prepared for her a sweet surprise, but how long can I endure?

Consuming me, amazing me, I feed off her hungry eyes

She makes it last, she makes us one, she makes the mountains rise

One look, one touch, and she's melting fast for me

Her kisses set my soul ablaze, as she slides down onto her knees

My fingers clutch her wild hair, she sets the beast inside me free

Her hungry eyes unlock the cage and then receives me openly

She wraps me in her summer and I glide upon her lake

I can't believe that she is real, this kind of passion you can't fake

For in a moment, in a flash, she pulls me in from far above

She's going to get everything I have, she's going to get all of my love

Do I Keep Up?

Do I keep up, baby?

Do I make you proud?

Do you feel me close when we are in a crowd?

You make me crazy

You make me sound

Each time we touch, I want to sing out loud

If there's a line we've crossed, that line's been lost

And there is nothing that can stop us now, our purpose is embossed

Past are all of the concerns that trust and hope be spurned

By the walking and the talking has our congress been confirmed

Do I keep up, baby?

Do I make you swoon?

Do you want to lie beside me under the dim light of the moon?

You make me crazy

You make my mood

And each time I withdraw, you rescue me from the cocoon

If there's a line we've crossed, that line's been lost

And there's nothing that can stop us now, our purpose is embossed

Past are all of the concerns that trust and hope be spurned

By the walking and the talking has our congress been confirmed

Not Alone

I know you're not alone tonight
You lie with flesh that is not mine
Not in my arms, but in my head
These fragile visions snap as twine

Will you not return this favor?
The gifts you give—why aren't they mine?
Not in my arms, but in my dreams
Magnets must, must not combine

I know you're not alone tonight
The senses filled will not be mine
Not in my arms, beneath my skin
Here lies the torment and cruelty of time

Waking Up

Weighted eyes with roaming mind
These restless nights been so unkind
You could not sleep or take a break
Those tears you've drained could fill a lake

But finally, you are waking up
You're getting more than you gave up
I'm here beside your new bedside
To fill the holes both deep and wide

Burdened heart with burning love
A tender reed, roots firm and tough
Yielding not to displaced thoughts
Life's victories are so hard-fought

But finally, you are waking up
You're getting more than you gave up
I'm standing here, come lean on me
Enjoy the free air that we breathe

Active hands and hopeful eyes
Your happiness uncompromised
And finally dreams now fill your sleep
Because you had the strength to leap

Finally, you have woken up
You're getting more than you gave up
I'm dreaming too, we lie as one
This new life for us just begun

She is Mine

She is this verse, which I transcribe
A feeling too hard to describe
My heart compelled by her heart's bribe
Pray to my verse will she subscribe

She is this wind that blows me by
She is my nighttime lullaby
And from her kiss comes her reply
Our passion clear, none can deny

She is a rock in troubled seas
The stars cast her abilities
Despite the shocks and frailties
I bask in her tranquilities

She is the forest's fawning bride
And in her hollow I will hide
Beneath the wood, I will confide
Defend her by my thick wolf's hide

Into the Deep

I circled down, into the deep
And in the depths, I found my feet
Firmed upon a mountain steep
I'll only fall if I don't leap

Upon the ledge, she holds my hand
In swirling, chilling wind we stand
Staring down upon dry land
We see ourselves and what we've planned

She's in my head; I feel her burning
The lore of love from youth returning
She feeds me when I need assuring
That to her my life is alluring

And now I've seen a fiery rose
The ends I do not presuppose
What we are nobody knows
My words for her themselves compose

When lovers meet, the stars align
But no omen gave us the time
Fate not cruel but clearly blind
The simple and complex will shine

I Wish

I wish I could write, and I wish I could sing
I wish I could give to you every good thing
But I can't, for I'm broken and the madness
I've spoken I've given you nothing

I wish I could dance, and I wish I could be
I wish that my love could bring you to your knees
But I can't, for I'm broken and these words but a token
Will we ever be free?

I wish I could speak, and I wish I could fly
I wish that you never had to wonder why
But I can't, for I'm broken, my lies pierce like a bodkin
It's torment when you cry

I wish that within, and I wish that without
I wish for contentment and never a doubt
But the world is so broken, and none left I can hope in
This silence makes me shout

Drift away and from afar
Come to me, wherever you are
Give to me your rolling tears
Let these scars not fate our years
Drift away and back again
Let not our music ever end

Aimless Ashes

Aimless white ashes surround me like snow
Each night that you leave me, more ashes do fall
Give me one night to give you my all
Give me one night, and inside you I'll crawl

You touch me, and I start to burn
To pleasure you is my one concern
You kiss me, you miss me, and I start to bleed
To open you up, my most pressing need

The faded ink lingers like ghosts on a page
Each day lived without you, more ink fades
Give me one night to give you me raw
Give me one night to taste what you are

You hold me tight as I start to grow
Your pleasure extends me and by this you know
You miss me, you kiss me, and I'm down on my knees
Come ride deep inside and find your ecstasy

Magic Place

She makes the world a magic place
Where in it neither time nor space
Stay her hand from spreading grace
She makes the world a magic place

She makes the hours of work fly by
Where in a building, see the sky
For such a love no fear to die
She makes the hours of work fly by

She makes the mundane seem serene
An hour with her ten in a dream
Her life is big, it fills the screen
She makes the mundane seem serene

She makes a simple man feel strong
He finally knows that he belongs
Important he amongst the throng
She makes a simple man feel strong

She turns each thought into a feat
A motivation to compete
Her skin so soft, her will concrete
She turns each thought into a feat

She makes the world a magic place
Where in it neither time nor space
Stay her hand from spreading grace
She makes the world a magic place

Magnets

My lover met me on a swing
She told me sweet and simple things
Her clever mind did us describe
And both our hearts felt a new vibe

What force compels a fateful day?
One path borne from two separate ways
What force could make the heavens form?
One star borne from two in the storm

Magnets repel, or they attract
Opposing strength, an immutable fact
Magnets repel, or they attract
Repelling bonds not meant to last

My lover met me on a hill
She took my hand, and time stood still
She made me feel, she kept her word
Upon that peak my song returned

What force can make the weary rise?
One love seen in two sets of eyes
What force can raise the living dead?
One mind borne from two spinning heads

Magnets repel, or they attract
Opposing strength, an immutable fact
Magnets repel, or they attract
Repelling bonds not meant to last

My lover saw my fractured past
Her love the light my stone heart cracked
My life a story short and long
I've seen the death and birth of dawn

What force can make the cells divide?
One life stronger than two half lives
What force makes lightning know its place?
One heart is born in time and space

Magnets repel, or they attract
Opposing strength, an immutable fact
Magnets repel, or they attract
Repelling bonds not meant to last

Happy Song

It started with a happy song
One that rhymed and was quite long
Some may claim it ordinary
Debate I will the contrary
For yes, it started merrily
Yet each turned page verily
Dove into the depths of mind
Where gold from stone was so refined
By the fire of pain and dread
All emotions have I bled
Into these minions that I bare
Incredible that I finally share
What was once hidden far from view
Such love and passion not I knew
Until the day she gripped my hand
From a slick ledge to dry land
The purest force to bend my ways
Covet I our precious days
Return I to these petty rhymes
Greatness not, but they are thine
Come join me on this weaving journey
May faith, love, joy replace the worries

My Best-Kept Secret

Whispers echo in my ears
Of her gentle voice I love to hear
All the secrets she has shared
She trusted me to treasure, she trusted me to care
On the seas I had been tossed
Upon her ivory coast, I found myself washed

She's my best-kept secret I've ever had
Every day I have to hide it is a day that drives me mad
She's my best-kept secret I'll ever keep
And the day she's not my secret is the day we took the leap

Riding on this fragile dream
Watching my sweet secret in her tight blue jeans
I watch her and follow close behind
Then grab and pin her to me to prove she's on my mind
Come let us rest upon the breeze
My little secret's glory brings me to bended knee

She's my best-kept secret I've ever had
Every day I have to hide it is a day that drives me mad
She's my best-kept secret I'll ever keep
And the day she's not my secret is the day we took the leap

Her Eyes, Her Eyes

Her eyes, her eyes, on they I'm sold
And like her spirit, they won't grow old
Though weary flesh may one day yield
Her eyes, her eyes, eternal fields

Like a concert, how they dance
The genesis of our romance
Though scoffers, they deny our chance
Her eyes, her eyes, are my advance

Her eyes mete truth, her heart is mine
Those mortal eyes touch the divine
As the hourglass drip grains of time
Her eyes, her eyes, as stars do shine

Tempt not I fate by hollow word
So much to say, my language blurred
By final line, I shall resolve
Her eyes, her eyes, are mine to love

Between

Between the crowd and pouring rain
She slips from me, my fingers strain
Between the shrouded, soaring days
I fill her with my vacant praise

Between the flicker of these lights
Under the sheets of sleepless nights
Between the winter and the spring
Her wispy voice so compelling

Her eyes, they sing
Her hands, they dance
Her gaze confirms this not by chance
Her eyes, they burn
Her voice, it quells
For her my secrets all will tell

Between the dead and newborn stars
A hardened heart and hope do spar
Between the head and true-born faith
The past, it haunts me like a wraith

Between the road and endless race
Our march propelled by each embrace
Between the want and needless needs
Are slain if her hand guarantees

Her eyes, they sing
Her hands, they dance
Her gaze confirms this not by chance
Her eyes, they burn
Her voice, it quells
For her my secrets all will tell

She's Burning

She's burning she's burning
Her world is turning
She knows her love she knows her love
She won't be left she will be loved

She stands apart she stands apart
She knows her love, she has his heart
She doesn't deserve what I have
I'll still give her everything that I have

She doesn't know all of me yet
She has my joy; can she take my regret?
Oh what love is this, what love is this?
It's new, it's fast, it could be missed

My love, my love is my only gift
It's weak and broken, it needs a lift
She's burning she's burning
Her world is turning

She needs the love she needs the love
My passion proves that she is loved
She will not be broken apart
She made me love, I'll save her with my reborn heart

Day was Long

The day was long, the hours thin

Would our love flourish; would it end?

My love was weary from the ride

Secrets buried deep inside

This little world that I had made

To be desired, to be craved

These the icons of my dreams

In a fit of childish screams

She stole them out upon the dark

Her passion journeyed, disembarked

I felt the truth behind her eyes

Simple, subtle, pure and bright

She waited there upon the shore

As darkness fell upon my floor

She called to me out of the mist

Her touch my life, I could subsist

Now all my days I owe her more

My love within you will endure

We walk upon the narrow trail

Together we will cross the veil

New Song

I want to sing a new song, new song
Sing it with me all day long, day long
Don't tell me that it's wrong, it's wrong
This is going to be our new song, new song

Baby, when you talk to me
Your eyes have tears, are they for me?
Baby, when you lay me down
You drive out all distracting sound

Baby, when you show me love
It's purer than a morning dove
Baby, when you share your grace
You wipe a smile right on my face

I want to sing a new song, new song
Sing it with me all day long, day long
Don't tell me that it's wrong, it's wrong
This is going to be our new song, new song

Baby, from the very start
You let me in your garden heart
Baby, from our first night out
I've never since had any doubt

Baby, from the night we kissed
In love with you I was convinced
Baby, from the time you turned
In fire we live but are not burned

I want to sing a new song, new song
Sing it with me all day long, day long
Don't tell me that it's wrong, it's wrong
This is going to be our new song, new song

You Make Me Special

You, you make me special
Over, under, everywhere you're quintessential
I'll follow you, just tell me where
I'll bare my soul, for it does care
You, you make me special

You, you make me better
Fortune, fame, or life forfeit I won't regret her
I'll carry you, just tell me where
My life for yours, use it with care
You, you make me better

You, you make us magic
Commit I this, our love will not fail or be tragic
I'll worship you, just say you care
Be with me here and everywhere
You, you make us magic

You, you make me special
Over, under, everywhere you're quintessential
I'll follow you, just tell me where
I'll bare my soul, for it do care
You, you make me special

Look at the Way

Look at the way she looks at me
Wet hair, bright eyes, sparkling
Never so active on a day inside
Soon I'll be back at her side

Look at the way she looks at me
Dress me like I'm modeling
Makes me want to make me more
Going deep, into my core

Coming is the day we won't be alone
Relegated not to our text-filled phones
This day is sure, for it's not unknown
How far we've come, how much we've grown

Look at the way she looks at me
Has me writing poetry
Each new verse gets to explain
Cleansing by her healing rain

Look at the way she looks at me
Sharing all life's complex scenes
Inspiration not a hassle
On a couch or in a castle

Coming is the day we won't be alone

Relegated not to our text-filled phones

This day is sure, for it's not unknown

How far we've come, how much we've grown

Heavens and Stars

You are the heavens, I your stars
And I'll light your night's sky till the end of time
You are the ocean, I your waves
And ceaseless desire will cause mountains to fall

You are an omen, I your prophet
And with your love, I'll make the faithless turn
You are the ends; may I be your means
And with your affection, impossible is no thing

You lift me and you turn me
You satisfy and spurn me
You fill me with obsession
You spark in me desire
My only ask don't leave me
Don't douse this fragile fire

You are a fortress, I your sentinel
And I'll guard our keep with unyielding eyes
You are beaming light, I your refraction
And the mirrors that we bear reveal what we cannot hide

You are the poet, I your lyric

And let not our inspiration sing about our grief

You are the temple, I your faithful servant

And let time not yield, our patience steel; our love must not forsake

You lift me and you turn me

You satisfy and spurn me

You fill me with obsession

You spark in me desire

My only ask don't leave me

Don't strand me on this wire

Voracity

We've explored this brave new country
Risen from the seas of uncertainty
You've gotten so close to me
But tell me, can you see?
All of me in you, and all of you in me

Our minds have slowly walked the line
Between the real and the sublime
I've gotten deep inside of you
But can you tell me, is it true?
All of me in you, and all of you in me

Baby, can't you feel my voracity
For what you give to me
All your intensity
And, baby, can't you slay my insecurity?
Can you feel my hand
Deep in a foreign land?

You charmed me like a velvet maiden
Your ivory skin is what I'm craving
I've turned you into part of me
Got lost in your insanity
All of me in you, and all of you in me

I'll wait on you, long sober hours

Through desert heat and typhoon showers

You've turned me into part of you

Will you tell me, is it true?

All of you in me, and all of me in you

Baby, can't you feel my voracity

For what you give to me

All your intensity

And, baby, can't you slay my insecurity?

Can you feel my hand

Deep in a foreign land?

Save Some Time for Me

Save some time for me
Wait patiently
Until I'm out of purgatory
Don't think that you're alone
All on your own
Your island will soon have company

You're my goal
I'm running, but life's quicksand is slowing me down
My heart's full
In seas of visions, I've slowly been drowned

Save some time for me
Instinctively
Let our two hearts weave intricately
Don't hang me on a line
Make us a crime
Our future worth waiting patiently

You're my goal
I'm running, but life's quicksand is slowing me down
My heart's full
In seas of visions, I've slowly been drowned

I Want

I want no other answer

I seek no other end

I want you as my lover

I need you as my friend

She's all that's crazy

She's all that I'll want

She gives me so much

But what more can I get?

Her eyes make me wild

Her skin makes me sweat

I want what she'll give me

But what more can I get?

Our Dimensions

Do our dimensions have intentions, or are they merely our inventions?

Will our dimensions drive contention; can they endure and have retention?

I do not deny us these dimensions

They have become our chief ambitions

Answers we seek shown to be

Our warp drive-powered gravity

Should our dimensions prove our mission, will fate accept new love's submission?

And if our dimensions relieve tensions, will this grant our hearts' permission?

I do not deny us these dimensions

They have become our chief ambitions

Answers seek we shown to be

Our warp drive-powered gravity

Birdsong

Sweep me off my feet

Draw me from the mire

From a pit reborn

Soft, your phoenix fire

Sing a birdsong new

Make a pact, entrust

Me with all your secrets

Till we dust to dust

Alas these symbols point

To meaning deep and pure

Despite the flesh travailing

By faith we can endure

Wonderful Thing

I sit here, and I try to scribe
The way you make this music vibe
These melodies have come alive
The moment that you got inside

I sit here trying to work out
The ways you turn my world about
And if you whisper or you shout
You'll be the lover that I tout

It's a wonderful thing
It's a wonderful thing
It's the reason you bring
You're the reason I sing

It's a wonderful thing
It's a wonderful thing
Every season is spring
When you accept my ring

A Phoenix soul is flowing gold, flowing gold, flowing gold. To a wolf her story told, bright and bold, bright and bold

Tonight

Tonight, I had wanted you all day
Tonight, there is no other way
Tonight, there is nothing left to say

Tonight, your fingers on my skin
Tonight, is the night you let me in
Tonight, is the way that we begin

Tonight, you opened up your soul
Tonight, you became my goal
Tonight, we lost control

I waited for tonight
I waited all my life
I'm ready for the fight
Tonight, I know it's right

Tonight, I took your trembling hand
Tonight, I vowed to by you stand
Tonight, we sleep on a fiery strand

Tonight, we found a way to sleep
Tonight, we dove into the deep
Tonight, you took this soul to squeeze

Tonight, we walked into the stars

Tonight, we shared our many scars

Tonight, your home between my arms

I waited for tonight

I waited all my life

I'm ready for the fight

Tonight, I know it's right

Together

Together, we are more than two
Together, we make old things new
Together, we are more than friends
Together, we can meet the ends

Together, we make ice and fire
Together, we burn with desire
Together, we sleep under stars
Together, we see near and far

Together, we light up the town
Together, we burn bridges down
Together, we make moments dear
Together, we sing loud and clear

Together, we can write these songs
Together, we make right our wrongs
Together, we can kiss and dance
Together, we make pure romance

So the Question Is

You have asked so many questions
You have challenged every move
You have charted the uncharted
Which you relentlessly pursued

You have pierced my outer shell
You have made your presence known
You have loosed the lava from the core
You drew water from dry stone

I have not repaid in kind
I apologize for this
But sit I here bemused
So the question is…

How do you know if it's something real?
How do you know if it's right to feel?
How do you know if it's going to seal?
How do you know if it's built from steel?

How do you know if it's right or wrong?
How do you know if you like this song?
How do you know if it's weak or strong?
How do you know if we both belong?

You have shown me with your eyes

You can make my mountains move

You must now accept and realize

There is nothing left to prove

Room at My Side

Lonely times like ocean waves
Every place looks just the same
Happiness is my greatest act
No love received have I given back

Relentless, repressing, reality
Unfazed by friends or family
Not one on which I can rely
No ally standing at my side

There's room by my side
I've waited patiently
There's room by my side
For you to rest on me

I won't complain or apologize
I made my island a paradise
But the days stretch like an endless beach
What I want now is within my reach

I do not seek their understanding
It's not their strip where I'll be landing
Someone listened and replied
An ally standing by my side

There's room by my side

I've waited patiently

There's room by my side

For you to rest on me

Let's Take a Walk

Baby, let's go take a walk
Let's find a quiet place to talk
We'll wander into forest green
And hide behind an old oak tree

Baby, let's go take a walk
Your prowling wolf protects his flock
I'll see that nature feels your grip
My heart, it pounds as the knot slips

Baby, let's go take a walk
Ascend we up a bloodied rock
A palace safe from desert's sun
A theater where we'll have some fun

Baby, let's go take a walk
Enjoy the sea, it never stops
Hand in hand, implore the stars
To be there as we fight our wars

I Need

I need your eyes, so I can see
I need your heart, oh hear it beat
I need your touch, for I am weak
I need your voice, so I can speak

Will you give me what I need
Or choke I on these tangled weeds?
Will you remain true to this creed?
Together we are what we need

I need your feet, so I can dance
I need your guidance to advance
I need your help to fix my stance
I need your luck to take this chance

I need your light, so I can write
I need your will to help me fight
I need you morning, day, and night
I need your truth, so I am right

Will you give me what I need
Or choke I on these tangled weeds?
Will you remain true to this creed?
Together we are what we need

Woke Up to You Talking

I woke up to you talking

And it made me feel so great

But then you slipped out the door

You took yourself away

You left me for the day

For another life to live

And I didn't have a thing to do but wait for your return

This isn't supposed to happen

Is it meant to be?

Without you, I drain quickly

I struggle sore and sickly

I fight this riot, sit here quiet

My emptiness, it's hard to hide it

I go silent, non-respondent

Make believe I'm not despondent

I watched you outside walking

The calm I felt made me melt

But you had to keep on moving

I knew this couldn't be

Your business just for me

Your kindness my remission

Worlds on course of collision, creeping through this small incision

This isn't supposed to happen

Is it meant to be?

Without you, I drain quickly

I struggle sore and sickly

I fight this riot, sit here quiet

My emptiness, it's hard to hide it

I go silent, non-respondent

Make believe I'm not despondent

My Fire

I at one time saw a fire
Across a glassy sea
Never so inspired
By banality

Wicked as I wandered
Uncertain, sullied ways
By madness could I ponder
My many wasted days

But back unto this fire
Which sailed upon my shore
My heart then learned desire
To fan it evermore

Waxing forms of distress
Suffer every soul
Castles, cages, kisses
Her heart mine, the goal

White flame purifying
Scarlet of my past
We will not stop trying
Death shall we outlast

Unbearable

It's unbearable
Lying all alone
With you on the phone
When are you coming home?

It's unbearable
In darkness, silence cries
Our moment's sweet surprise
Left longing for your eyes

It's unbearable
Without you, nothing moves
You rock me, set my groove
And there's nothing left to lose

It's unbearable
The sinking
The constant overthinking
You give this man his purpose
And deliver him his confidence

Run to a Place

Run to a place, running to an end
Running in a field, where the sunlight never dims
Pick up the pace, picking up the beat
Picking up the tab, so the party doesn't sleep

There is a howl, calling in the wild
Calling to my baby, to my little baby child
Answer the call, answering the voice
Answering her call because there is no other choice

If you had what I had
Would you give it up?
Would you give up to the right?
Or descend into the night?

If you had what I had
Would you let it go?
Would you give up in a fight?
Or take her home tonight?

My Duty

It's my duty to find a perfect new line
Find another way and a relevant rhyme
All my mind is set on you
Making you mine

What do I do when I have the time?
Paint a picture and make you shine
Will you let me inside you?
Changing your mind

Your love like the waters bring life
This dry desert sunshine is making me blind
Here you are all around me
Surrounding my skies

It's my duty to blaze a new trail
One made of stone, one that won't fail
I will always sweat for you
Laying down this rail

Little Light

This nascent light of mine
You hold it in your heart
And from your eyes it shines

This fragile light of mine
No matter where you hide
I'll find, I'll free your mind

I've sung my song of sadness
I've made a pact with madness
You've lifted up my countenance
Let me fill you with this romance

This growing light of mine
You share it with the world
And from your hands it shines

This flaming light of mine
You hide it in your heart
It thrives within your ivory vines

I've sung my song of sadness
I've made a pact with madness
You've lifted up my countenance
Let me fill you with this romance

Bring Me Down

Baby, won't you help me come back down
I've been spinning around, running aground
Baby, won't you make it so it hurts no more
I've been limping along, writing this song

Come on, baby, bring me down
My head's been in the clouds, I can't touch the ground
Come on, baby, bring me down
You've lifted me up, and now I can't make a sound

Baby, won't you help me come back down
I've been lost in the woods, up to no good
Baby, won't you take me to another place
I've been floating through space, I can't finish the race

Come on, baby, bring me down
My head's been in the clouds, I can't touch the ground
Come on, baby, bring me down
You've lifted me up, and now I can't make a sound

You've been making me feel solid
You've been driving my ambition
I'm going to make you call my name
Make you feel a new sensation

Come on, baby, bring me down

My head's been in the clouds, I can't touch the ground

Come on, baby, bring me down

You've lifted me up, and now I can't make a sound

Winter-Born

She is winter-born
She came out of a storm
In sunless skies, she shone
A vacant wood no more alone

Soft the untouched snow
Above the white, she floats
Her blood-red lips do glow
Against the starlit snow

A child of nature, she
Mother's novelty
On ice her travels be
Between the alpine trees

Her grace forms many shapes
Like countless falling flakes
In dress of crystal draped
Her open hands, the snow creates

She is winter-born
Her cry the season's horn
The silence never torn
As to peace, her life is sworn

Something New

A walk along an endless trail

The hapless shade my sorrow

The hope that hope might just prevail

It sleeps upon the morrow

There are few times I've felt this way

Life's tenor oh so dreary

A beast trapped in a narrow cage steals rest, my soul so weary

Then comes a day when darkness falls

It shatters like a mirror

As evening draws, my lover calls

Her light dispels the terror

This is your gift, though it is mine

Your affection, my desire

Timeless words cannot define how my phoenix bears the fire

It's hard to grant what you deserve, and I want to oh so dearly

What little tokens, all my nerve, the scanner it sees clearly

Far Come

Good morning there, my burdened girl
What thoughts inside your head now swirl?
It's early, but I know you're thinking
Don't let that ship of joy go sinking

Here we are, we've come so far
Making sense between the bars
Circumstances locked in jars
Keeping fresh the wins and scars

Good morning there, my merry girl
Living in the wind and whirl
Buffered by that pleasant smile
Tell me, will it go the mile?

Here we are, we've come so far
Weathered by our many wars
Vessels born in fire and tar
Stretching out beyond the stars

Is It Easier to Love Me?

Is it easier to love me, if I hide away my heart?

Can I take you to that secret place, even if it's dark?

Would you take my hand and hold it, through the briars of my mind?

Living in me is a spirit neither feeling, neither blind

Is it easier to love me, if I only show one face?

Would you want to be my lady, only if I gave thee chase?

Do you want me to live freely or confine me to your space?

Living in me is a spirit only wanting to make waste

Is it easier to love me, if I lead you by the hand?

Will you only ever trust me if I admit that I am damned?

Can you lie with me and smile without a saintly reprimand?

Living in me is a spirit I'm not sure I can withstand

Learned

I've lived a simple life
Made some friends, took a wife
Witnessed children from my flesh
Felt the worst, seen the best
I've been down country roads
Seen some come, seen some go
Watched the eyes before they closed
One last song in mind arose

How does one know what is real?
Earth and sky do not reveal
What can prove a heart exists?
Be it a wolf or a phoenix?

I've chosen many paths
Some of mercy, others wrath
Turned a blind eye to my sin
Shades of gray, colors blend
I've seen another world
Through the glass, stained and blurred
Seen the final breath of man
From flesh the soul disbanded

How does one know what transcends?
Quarrels kill the best of friends
Purposeful or parlor tricks?
Rests in the eye of the phoenix

I've made a single pact
Make a vow, get attacked
Remand me to this dream
It escapes, if you're seen
I've sacrificed my heart
Secret places, hidden parts
Into the deep, I've leapt
In me is my one love's heart kept

I can tell them now what's real
It's not what you know, but what you feel
I can tell them what transcends
A phoenix that her wolf defends

Take the Time to Write It Down

Take the time to write it down
Don't let them out to sea and drown
To let her know you love her sound
Take the time to write it down

Take the time to write it down
Hum a tune till words are found
Bring drifting passions to the ground
Make her smile and make her proud

Take the time to write it down
Cut the cord, unleash the hounds
In her eyes, love will abound
Just because you wrote it down

She

See where she stands, like soft reeds in wet sand
I'm not alone
She moves the water, and I no longer falter
Again

She took me by the hand and took me to another land
And I'm not afraid that she will let me go
She's made my heart yield to all was once concealed
Now it's easier for her to let me know

She dresses daylight like rivers dance with moonlight
A song
She paints the skyline like bright green winter pines
I'm hers alone

She took me by the hand and took me to another land
And I'm not afraid that she will let me go
She's made my heart yield to all was once concealed
Now it's easier for her to let me know

May this joy song never end, all my worries she transcends
What she wants revealed, I will show
For her love always defends, never waivers, never bends
May she come to me and never let me go

What Happy Makes

Sitting and dreaming up some lines
Reflecting to find meaning
Blurred have become our separate lives
You get my heart fast beating

You make it bright
You make it fight
I make it wrong; you make it right
I soon will break; I will forsake
For baby, you're what happy makes

Oh child, can't you turn and see
I'm sitting by you singing
All day long, you're after me
Love to my heart you're feeding

You make it bright
You make it fight
I make it wrong; you make it right
I soon will break; I will forsake
For baby, you're what happy makes

Come and fulfill this poor man's dream
He smiles when he sees you
You're going to always make me scream
I'll give you my life as proof

You make it bright
You make it fight
I make it wrong; you make it right
I soon will break; I will forsake
For baby, you're what happy makes

Moments

We have our moments, I relive
Each time we fight, we each forgive
Each time we love, the passion spreads
We walk inside each other's treads

We have our long and patient meals
Each time we chase each other's heels
Each time we merge it heats the fire
We are become each one's desire

We have our evenings in the air
Each time we walk up endless stairs
Each time we doubt we show our faith
We fasten to each one's embrace

Cheer

You ran to me
When I was at my weakest
You took my hand
And led me out of the pit

Your love for me
In me, it is the deepest
Your charity
I promise to protect it

Cheer for me, cheer for us
Even if we can't, we must
Fall for me, fall for us
Even though it's hard to trust

You sang to me
When I needed to recover
You called me up
To tell me it's okay

Your love, you shared
And my spirit found its lover
You're coming home
In my arms, I'll keep you safe

Cheer for me, cheer for us

Even if we can't, we must

Fall for me, fall for us

Even though it's hard to trust

Thankful

Thankful am I for my girl
And all those ways she spins and twirls
How I rise by her first light
And find my way to sleep at night

Thankful am I for my muse
And all her shops I do peruse
How I move on her command
And ransom all that she demands

Thankful am I for my friend
And her dimensions I transcend
How I fly with her broad wings
And swim within her brilliant springs

Waking Up the Pen

This pen has remained silent
For lo these many years
The heart lay uninspired
No cause for joy, no pause for tears

But the first time that I saw her
I felt the winds of change draw near
Like a light that's just been wired
Her voice was ringing in my ears

Waking up to a new morning
Unlike any one before
Waking up, no longer mourning
A regrown forest to explore
Waking up to find new meaning
In everything I once ignored
Waking up with my face beaming
For the one whom I adore

Today this pen is brilliant
And cannot be stayed or stowed
Now a heart unchained is longing
For the love that she's bestowed

A resurgence of my passion
An emergence of pure grace
I will write forevermore
To put a smile on her face

Waking up to a new morning
Unlike any one before
Waking up, no longer mourning
A regrown forest to explore
Waking up to find new meaning
In everything I once ignored
Waking up with my face beaming
For the one whom I adore

Our Castle

To build a castle, no small feat
The work begins when soulmates meet
And from the time of our first kiss
Our castle grew out of the mist

Each stone a trial we've survived
Curtain walls, us side by side
The courtyard lined with sprawling vines
Adorned with roses and soft pines

Thick mortar our fidelity
Tall spires our spirits both set free
Firm buttresses our two hearts weaved
Our castle overlooks the sea

Deep moat is trust by which we live
Strong keep our power to each forgive
Court jesters make our joys relive
Our castle strong on jagged cliffs

When our two hearts congressed as one
Our castle born beneath the sun
A fairy tale had we begun
Till ever after, our kingdom

Mine eyes behold thy wings of gold, to fire my soul is sold, and finally have I found my name as drift I down into thy flame

Red Stone

Red-faced stones and sprawling pines
Snowcapped peaks placed in a line
Nature had so much to share
But only you could hold my stare

Despite the cold crisp morning ride
Up through an endless mountainside
I could not see but one bright star
In this our little red train car

My love, she sat there next to me
The only thing I'd want to see
Despite a peak two miles high
She was the object in my eye

We talked we laughed, we soared we sighed
We spent the journey side by side
We wondered what would make us whole
To be together was the goal

And rocks that grew out of the plains
Surrounded us while dreams explained
Our life and love, if normalcy
Would we ward off complacency?

Hours rounding, bounding trails
Hand in hand, two hearts set sail
Longing to both drop the veil
With faith our love will never fail

In our travels came our song
No longer were our minds withdrawn
Together must we be the strong
And merry we the whole day long

MMXVI

Long and slothful hours
Stretch out these lonely days
Like winding stairs up towers
A struggle either way
I could simply say I miss you
But that won't sum it up
Our passion a volcano
Together we erupt
With vivid colors painting
This blind canvas gets sight
We touch, it's elevating
Inspires us to fight

You are such a beauty
Earth's wonders a mirage
These few years left, my duty
To paint thee a collage
Pen strokes of adoration
Reflecting, I'll proclaim
That you're the incarnation
Of fiery grace, untamed
I've heard so many love songs
But all this they lack
The parts of love the strongest
Are found between the cracks

Here, a new star forming
Within this sky of mind
Frightening and warming
Both fear and faith are blind
Time spent recollecting
On how we got to now
Continually inspecting
Each memory a cloud
Many shapes are blending
Into a vision clear
Distractions contending
As mist upon life's mirror

Short and blissful hours
Oft hurried, lovely days
One castle many towers
Upon bedrock were they raised
Soft, angelic chorus
Morning stars, your two eyes
Greatness here before us
Perfection, I surmise
Conclusions, concluding
Deep roots in wind may sway
One truth not eluding
Toward eternity, we blaze

I Felt You Yesterday

I felt you yesterday
Your lips had much to say
I love the way they play
Lay me down, take me away

I felt you yesterday
Let come whatever may
I'm not going to betray
Build the heat like the midday

I felt you yesterday
My fingers in the hay
You took me where I lay
Your gift I will repay

What I Write

What I write, you let me read
You say you love what you see
When we kiss, I must concede
You draw love's whisper out of me

What you grant me is this trance
From which there is no wealth or fame
Is it circumstance or romance?
When there's no one left to blame

What makes me feel so joyous?
It's your subtle swirling stare
Which makes me feel victorious
That my cares no longer care

What I try to state with clarity
Comes out often muddled
Please take this pauper's charity
May it leave you not befuddled

What I share is born from pain
And you do not turn your eye
I pray my hope is not in vain
That you could love this weak reply

I Hope You Know

I hope you know I love you
The sunrise won't rise up before you
If I dream at night, it's about you
I hope you know I love you

I hope you know I love you
No time or place can deny you
Everything I write is about you
I hope you know I love you

I hope you know I love you
My planets revolve all around you
All these words pour out for you
I hope you know I love you

What I Want Is Not Mine

What I want is not mine
I did not seek, but I did find
Now my heart commits a crime
Better had I remained blind

Never thought to never mind
Dazzled as her bright eyes shined
Needed to respond in kind
Her home the place beyond the pines

Wayward drawn by skin so fine
Her smile a gift from the divine
She the path that is my line
Walk it I till end of time

My Little Lady

These wounds that never seemed to heal
Entombed in a weary world until
That day when suddenly I found my eye
That day when she came into my life

Monsoons that once flooded by mind
Just dreams, my Hawkmoon 269
Then she looked at me with those eyes
Then she reversed the course of time

My, oh my little lady
Came she here to save me
My, oh my little lady
Can she finally change me?

These scars, they always remember
Those parts, which haunt us until
That day when she stood by my side
That day when she became my pride

Snow storms that once whitewashed my mind
In dreams, no rose could I find
Then she looked at me with those eyes
Then she pulled my soul to her side

My, oh my little lady

Came she here and saved me

My, oh my little lady

Did she finally change me?

When It's Your Time

You made a pact, did not retract
When trouble came, you had my back
And trouble now is at your door
It is the time to test your core

When it's your time
Go shine go shine
Don't let the doubts your will unbind
When it's your time
You'll find you'll find
True rest comes after a long grind

You took a step, on the precept
That to the change you are adept
And now it's time to take a stand
Knowing that I'm your biggest fan

When it's your time
Go shine go shine
Don't let the doubts your will unbind
When it's your time
You'll find you'll find
True rest comes after a long grind

My Song

My song is here because you sang
Your voice echoes deep in my brain
I hear, I see, I feel, I know
You are from whence all blessings flow

Take this hand before it fades
From our past our future saved
We struggled through the stormy times
And here we stand, hearts intertwined

The more I drift, the more I see
How full you filled these holes in me
I taste, I touch, and I believe
If you are mine, no more to achieve

Take this hand before it fades
Work I hard for passing grade
On altars have we sacrificed
In death our love has found its life

My song is here because you sang
Your voice echoes deep in my brain
I hear, I see, I feel, I know
You are from whence all blessings flow

Sweet Verse

There is a sweet verse

Hummed deep inside me

I'm going to break free

And sing softly in your ears

There is a joy song

A tiny playground

Ride on the sweet sound

Magic the ground beneath her feet

Love me for me, love

Take all of me, love

Come set me free, love

Love raise the ladder, rescue me

I found a high note

Up on a mountain

Soft like a fountain

Come take this trail along with me

There is a cool wind

Across the highland

Shared with my best friend

My love finally delivered me

Love me for me, love

Take all of me, love

Come set me free, love

Love raise the ladder, rescue me

Count

Count to one, count to two

Give me the confidence that I can count on you

Count to one, count to two

Make it to three, and let love deliver you

I will find your hidden places; you can count on me to try

If you hide from me, your heart will crack and break apart inside

You can count on me to let you be and let you let it out

You can thank me later for those days I spun your world about

Count to one, count to two

Light a signal flare, and I'll come to rescue you

Count to one, count to two

Make it to three, and you'll see our love is true

I will find your hidden places; you can count on me to try

If you hide from me, your heart will crack and break apart inside

You can count on me to let you be and let you let it out

You can thank me later for those days I spun your world about

Count to one, count to two

Let me say it once again that I'm in love with you

Count to one, count to two

Make it to three, and put all of me in you

Be My Burden

Don't hide from me when you hurt
Don't think I cannot bear it
Loving you is all I want to do
My shoulder is your altar

Be my burden, be my weight
I'll free you, open your gate
Be my burden, be my chain
I'll set you loose; I'll cut the reins

Look at me and share your tears
I'll share with you the pain
Don't think I cannot hold your hand
Even while you're pulling away

Be my burden, be my weight
I'll free you, open your gate
Be my burden, be my chain
I'll set you loose; I'll cut the reins

I am yours; will you trust in my love?
I am in color now because of you
Don't refrain, for passion we will sustain
Release your pain, and know I'll do the same

Be my burden, be my weight

I'll free you, open your gate

Be my burden, be my chain

I'll set you loose; I'll cut the reins

My Love

My love's a flame of burning stone
She yields not to temporal tones
For her, it's real or it's a lie
And her faith, once sworn, cannot deny

My love's a shield to what life throws
She protects me from slings and arrows
For time with her is a blessing
And her testament is impressing

My love's a song that never ceases
She cures my heart from its diseases
For who could stay the hand of time?
She sends kind thoughts into my mind

My love's a rain that ends the drought
She purifies pain and cleanses doubt
For her, my soul forced to be stronger
And for her, pray my life grants longer

My love's a painting which hangs serene
She is a crown jewel to be seen
By her I'm born out of the rift
Her grace and love in time won't shift

My love's the tower that looms beyond
She from great distance ties the bond
For with my heart laid on the altar
I know she will not fail or falter

My love's the shade in the heat of day
She's by my side and doesn't stray
For she keeps her grace in an infant vial
From heart to lips, there's no denial

My love's a bell, and with every hour
She bares her soul, I feel its power
For with her, I won't fear my weakness
Her light dispels the black and bleakness

My love's the truth, like a gospel song
She sings it for me all day long
For we were chosen for a reason
To deny this, both lie and treason

My love's a choice and all that's free
She is my bliss and serenity
For her, I'll chase down all good words
And will not rest till she is heard

My love's a tree which flowers dress
She brings forth what has been repressed
For now her radiance glows so starkly
I finally see through glass once darkly

Such as I Have

Silver and gold, I do not have
Yet the loveliest creature before me stands
With me she's happy; it's hard to believe
How much her touch in me can relieve

What can I say that's not meaningless?
Each time we talk I have more to confess
I don't have the fame or the clout to require
May this, my song, be all you desire

Such as I have, I give to thee
A taste of my mind's best poetry
For what I write, it comes with ease
Know that you have my soul to please

Such as I have, I give to thee
And nothing can stop the insanity
But before I fall to bended knee
Accept this gift of my gaiety

Such as I have, I give to thee
Pray be my song your prosperity
Learned have I by your third degree
That magnets are bound by polarity

What I Feel

I feel myself departing from what my life's print was imparting

Then her kindling, fire sparking, set the sails by which I'm charting

And I feel with every moment in time spent discontented

When she leaves me, leaves me longing, like a sin gone unrepented

Now I see the night sky lighting when she walks into the room

Her eyes in mine the eye of God, resurrecting this my tomb

And I feel that one word wasted by such menial expression

That before I dare to use it, be it born from my obsession

And I feel you make me wander woods that others merely ponder

Could this be true, my trust that you know I'm your one responder

So many words, and many more, I'll scour to paint this image

On an ivory tower I found my power through her unsullied visage

I feel you feel, and you make me feel, I no longer should avoid

That within, without, and all about you've helped me touch the void

I have this poetry in my mind, but like the fog it's fading

To give you this, my damaged thought, is what I've been debating

I seek a dream from not to wake, the only sleep I dare to take

To seek and find what can unbind, a search I won't forsake

I feel relief, but no reprieve; what expectations to believe

If you were mine, a dream divine, what could we not achieve?

I suffer hours all alone, it's painful like a venom

The whirling, twirling sands of time escape us as we live them

Rest, my angel, as thy wings reflect twilight like diamond rings

Soft you now, the sweetest thing—see what you've wrought from this wellspring

Ropes

The ropes wrapped 'round her
Tightening as she struggled
Were they to suffocate or secure?
Then one day she met a man
He could see these ropes around her
She tried to hide them, but he knew
He took the work to break them loose
One by one. the ropes did snap
With each that fell, she found more strength
But as the ropes tore, so she was torn asunder
Freedom bears the weight of risk
She thanked the man but still accused
For without him, she would still be bound
Faith she learned came from sure hope
She was sure she loved this man
Without bonds, she felt cool air
Took to flight above the sorrows below
When run to ground to find the path
Thorny trails are those less traveled
Trials separate the faithful and expedient
Her strength made new a peerless cord
Bound to her side, bound to his side
In fire they stood to forge the bond
She was sure she loved this man

Your Words

Your words can make me high
Your words can paint the sky
Your words feel like a lie
Your words, they make me sigh
Your words my lullaby
Your words I can't deny

You are an everything
My heart skips, my soul sings
Just like the butterfly
Your words can make me fly

Your words are soft and pure
Your words they reassure
Your words do so allure
Your words in me endure
Your words make my path sure
Your words make me secure

You are an everything
My heart skips, my soul sings
Just like the crying wolf
Your words my poor heart soothes

Your words make my tears dry

Your words can make me cry

Your words will make me try

Your words are semper fi

Your words I can rely

Your words never defy

For You Are Good

For you are good
It makes it easy for me to say
For you are good
It means God answers when I pray

You are so real
You make me feel
My thoughts you steal
My wounds you heal

For you are good
I can find these words to write
For you are good
These feelings I don't have to fight

You are a dream
You're filling reams
My eyes, they beam
These fingers scream

For you are good
I don't have to be shy
For you are good
I'll hold you close until I die

We Wander

Upon the cliffs, we wander
Then suddenly underwater
Side by side, we slip away
Drifting toward new shore

Washed upon a golden beach
Hand in hand but out of reach
Staring out across the bay
Seeing so much more

Walk across the fertile isle
All things new as to a child
Sunlight makes a better day
Better than before

All the work to make love real
Why to most it's not revealed
Love it not the simple way
Let us find the door

Flower

Oh, how I love to be inspired
Sadly, it comes when I'm tired
And before I can express
My mind yields to sweet rest
One may say I'm rather weary
Battling the bleak and bleary
But before I fall depressed
My little flower finds me rest

She is a rose and all her petals
Glow so bright like painted metal
No matter how my body tires
My little flower always inspires
Perched atop her rolling hill
To live in her world is a thrill
Her colors fast, her colors deep
And when I reach her, I can sleep

Oh, how I love to be inspired
Unto my study, I've retired
In the warm light find my place
My flower puts my heart to race
Against the hours passing quickly

Wish my wit was far less sickly

Seeking ways to show my flower

That she is my source of power

Need

Her eyes bled red from the ceaseless tears
Building lo these many years
Her mind paced, raced, from the endless drain
One path simple, one path faith

Her incipient angel, though he be dark
Waited for her hand, loved her from the start
Her recipient angel, though he be weak
Gave to her his heart, wings cast to her feet

Her heart jumped pumped from true passion's force
Uttered vows are not joy's source
Her skin felt, melts, from his solid grip
Taste the honey on his lips

Her incipient angel, though he be dark
Waited for her hand, loved her from the start
Her recipient angel, though he be weak
Gave to her his heart, wings cast to her feet

We Owe Each Other Nothing

We owe each other nothing
So we give each other everything
The defining of our being
Is to make each other freeing

Let not we taunt the time we share
Each hour flees as if it's scared
Though patient we within the snare
How much more time apart can we bear?

Blessed are we by bright assurance
Our love has strength and endurance
To make it through what seems deterrence
We know that we are no recurrence

Complements

I am happy, you are sad
You are peaceful, I am mad
I am prim, you aren't proper
You are go, I'm the stopper

You and I are complements
Time with you is time well spent
When we touch we feel that pull
With each other we are full

I am rich, you are poor
You withdraw, I want you more
I greet day, you call night
You are certain, I am right

You and I are complements
Stolen moments, sacraments
When we walk we feel that joy
Our castle built can't be destroyed

I am mercy, you are grace
You make stars, I have space
I am yours, you are mine
You are a spark, I see divine

You and I are complements

This poem hereby documents

Our lives these lyrics represent

You and I are complements

Vision

You came to me and stayed awhile
A vision had your mind compiled
Explained to me a new dimension
Where we could live without the tension
In this place, they all knew our name
And praised us for our love proclaimed
A village where we both could thrive
A world in which we could survive

The moonlight robbed our precious time
And stole from us this world sublime
Swore we both unto a mission
The vision's vision our retention
Such agony these severed lives
Each day we walk on edge of knives
Now to dreams we're relegated
Until our vision is created

My Eyes Be Blind

My eyes be blind, but I'm seeing clear
Holding tight to what's so dear
Making time to let her know
She's the spotlight in my show

Now, going to make her mine
Now, is our time to shine
Grapes of wrath we turn to wine
Rest with me, for we are fine

I hear this verse, falling with the rain
Cleaning off immature stains
She the kind the mind would trick
Show her love in thin and thick

Now, going to make her turn
Now, is our time to burn
Watch this poet make her cry
Then wipe each teardrop from her eyes

It may be brief, but I hope she's heard
Inside of me life has stirred
For her hand I'd cross the Nile
Every day I'll make her smile

Now, going to make her want

Now, writing in new font

Sailing past, the ruins fading

Take my hand and stop debating

Providence

When you are not looking, but suddenly you see a face

When you are not trying, but finally you find your place

The unexplained

The desert rains

Catching the last midnight train

Her name is Providence, Providence

When you are not rolling, but somehow you have won the game

When you are not assured, but then one day you know your name

The forest fire

The inner choir

Rebirth of the inner child

Her name is Providence, Providence

My love, she came one day

When I was looking the other way

Oh love, she is a mystery

Providence, she stands in front of me

I Think of Things

I think of things I want to do
For you, with you, to you, through you
I think of things I've made you see
For me, with me, to me, through me

We are two, a pair of kinds
We shine bright, above the pines
Starry night, Van Gogh'd be proud
We the song that lifts the shroud

I think of things I want to be
Because of you I've been set free
I think of things in shades of blue
My earth reborn, my life anew

We are two, an unmatched pair
We repel the world's despair
Count the ways, make Browning sing
Our hearts forged, a golden ring

Poet Out of Me

You're going to make a poet out of me
By painting pictures of our memories
Don't act surprised; it's not a mystery
I think of you, and my heart writes poetry

You make me feel like I have the mastery
To touch your soul and heart collectively
My words like water flow effortlessly
From dusk till dawn, I'm swarmed by similes

I used to hide away so cautiously
You made my heart race oh so speedily
Like a flock of birds guided back from sea
My mind your home to live in comfortably

You've gone and made a poet out of me
I hope you know it's not a novelty
My mind because of you has been set free
I think of you, and my heart writes poetry

Can You Tell Me?

Can you tell me why?

Can you tell me how?

Can you tell me when?

Cause I want you now

Can you talk to me?

Can you make me smile?

Can you stay with me

For a little while?

All these things

And many more

You've made them mine

And opened my door

All these things I do adore

You've calmed me down

You've made me yours

Can you dance for me?

Can you play along?

Can you let me be

While I right the wrong?

Can you sit with me?
Can you stay out late?
Can you pass the time
Till we celebrate?

All these things
And many more
You've made them mine
And opened my door
All these things
I do adore
You've calmed me down
You've made me yours

A Place

Between two worlds a lady torn
An oath to break to be reborn
One place of joy
One place of fear
A path well-worn is oft unclear

Without regret expressed her will
Sheep scatter when the wolves draw near
No place to run
No place to hide
How does the child inside survive?

From confidence is born resolve
With faith the certainty of love
The place she saw
The place to fly
Her freedom glimmered in blue sky

To change the course of one's own life
One must be prepared for the strife
A place to fight
A place to die
The phoenix spread her wings to fly

Surviving Charades

I never want to know a life
Where you are not the one
By my side, by my side
Confidence once petrified
Suffered alone while I
Swallowed pride, swallowed pride

I want to take you away
Far away, far away
I want tomorrow today
Far away, far away

And all the games we must play
Find a way, find a way
Surviving charades
Find a way, find a way

Together we can walk the knife
Make fate lovely as we
Turn the tide, turn the tide
Confidence solidified
Purpose that my love be
Satisfied, satisfied

I want to take you away

Far away, far away

I want tomorrow today

Far away, far away

And all the games we must play

Find a way, find a way

Surviving charades

Find a way, find a way

Today

Today's the day you're coming home
This joy I feel nobody's known
Tonight I know that I'll sleep through
All dreams I have are dreams of two

Two of us to rule our world
One shy boy and one strong girl
Two of us to change the time
A man to make his diamond shine

I love you, yes, I love you, ma'am
Come to me and take my hand
Walk with me and wait awhile
You gave to me this endless smile

Write I a song with ease these days
With many words, no way to phrase
Just how much you mean to me
Filled am I by you with glee!

My Life for Yours

My life for yours

That's what I'll say

I love you

Weak, in every way

For love is an idea blurry

My life for yours I would not worry

My life for yours

In this new year

I love you

Won't remove the fears

For love is a temporal fate

My life for yours at heaven's gate

My life for yours

That's my vow

I love you

Can't repel fate's howl

For love will move along with time

My life for yours a final line

My life for yours

An immutable pact

I love you

Is a transient fact

For love may waver in the dark

My life for yours is true love's spark

What You Make

You make me so much bigger
Larger than my life
We laugh like best of friends
We love like man and wife

You make me so much stronger
Built for troubled times
We make each other better
We reach for the divine

You are a magic woman
Clever, kind, and wise
We run like wolves in winter
Under the starlit skies

You make me see the seasons
Gold and white and green
We see none but each other
We share the same sweet dream

You make your man a writer
His poet song for thee
We wander peaks and valleys
We float upon the breeze

Oh My

Oh my oh my, this glass is mine
Behind the veil bright diamonds find
Would all the sparks of heaven shine
No more on God's good grace I'd bind

Oh my oh my, this wild flame grows
It's faith in temperature doth show
That most of life we poor men go
Until we rest in beauty's glow

Inward turn my eyes to verse
The better I within these burst
Forth from sweet joy from whence we're born
Oh my oh my, to her I'm sworn

Oh my oh my, I hear her voice
And must I now confirm this choice
Declare my love, her pure flag hoist
May all angels with wings rejoice

Oh my oh my, I write a song
A song to sing the whole day long
And when my days no more be strong
Her love for me drives out all wrongs

Inward, outward vacillate

Her with me doth make me great!

And for her hand I do await

All wounds, all fears she dissipates

Sit with Me

Sit with me come sit with me
Tell me what you need
Sit with me come sit with me
I'll be beside your side
Trust in me come trust in me
Let your love roll in let it all come in
Eternity is near to me
You made my start and will be my end

And all and all I can see are your eyes
And all and all I can give is my life
If you sit with me if you stay with me
Fall with me and pray with me
I'll never seek another's hand
I'm whole I'm whole

Sit with me come sit with me
Tell me what you need
Sit with me and stay with me
I'll defend you till I die
Trust in me come trust in me
Let your arms fall down let your life abound
Eternity is near to me
You made my start and will be my end

And all and all I can see are your eyes
And all and all I can give is my life
If you sit with me if you stay with me
Fall with me and pray with me
I'll never seek another's hand
I'm whole I'm whole

*My love a flame for thee I burn
and from thine ashes I'll return*

Mythics

Two mythics met and made a pact
A sacred vow not to retract
One a beast of woodland fame
The other borne by death and flame
This purpose have I to regale
Our reader with this lovers' tale
So let us share their story brief
Their mythic love defies belief

A hunter with gold haunting eyes
In packs their strength be realized
The deep cold air can't breach their fur
When they give chase tis but a blur
Of gray and black and brown and white
Dark colors lighting up the night
The sharpened claws and padded paws
The danger of their snarling jaws
But when they love it's with their lives
Devotion is how they survive
No beast is this with wing or hoof
One mythic was a lonely wolf

They regal red with ruby eyes

Their fiery hearts melt hearts of ice

Neither tame and neither wild

Defend their master as their child

Perched upon a wizard's post

Shrouded by history's ghosts

For time a storm they all must weather

No scars of age upon their feather

And when they love, it's bittersweet

As mortals fall before their feet

Their endless flame revives the sick

The other mythic a phoenix

One may not see how this became

A story meriting such fame

Yet one dark cold and lonely night

This wolf and phoenix met in moonlight

Our wolf upon the chase got lost

No family to fight off the frost

The frigid night like none before

This wolf was moving toward death's door

And by magic or by miracle

The Phoenix heard the wolf's weak calls

Taking flight into the storm

The snow like wasps around her swarmed

The wolf, he stumbled in deep snow
His spirit slowly letting go
The cold now creeping to his heart
His eyes grew dim to match the dark
But just before he closed his eyes
He heard a song up in the skies
No strength to lift his heavy head
His golden eye saw something red
Like a ball of fire in the sky
A falling star flew to his side
The wolf, his head fell to the snow
A light he saw though his eyes closed

The phoenix could not bear the pain
Her glowing eyes dripped tears of flame
This beast so lovely could not die
Then felt she love, it burned inside
In moments she was so engulfed
The flames must save this freezing wolf
The frozen snow began to yield
The forest floor finally revealed
But stopped not she until sunrise
And when the wolf opened his eyes
She knew she'd saved him from the mire
Then consumed was she by her fire

The massive wolf slowly arose
A circle 'round him had no snow
And centered in this warm dry patch
There stood a little pile of ash
He tarried there to understand
How was it he now on dry land?
His memory had been so marred
What happened in this field so charred?
It then came to him suddenly
A sacrifice had set him free
And vowed he to defend her mark
No creature here would ever walk

He no longer needed his pack
For to her had he made this pact
Then one night as the wolf slept by
The pile of ash against his hide
Felt he a warmth and turned his head
To see the ash like embers red
And in a moment, in a flash
No more was there a pile of ash
For in its place there stood his grace
The creature had taken his place
His blazing eyes pierced to her soul
And looking back, she saw his gold

There were no words they need exchange

For what they felt, the gods arranged

A wolf and phoenix may seem absurd

But what makes sense is rarely heard

For love is more than fire and ice

It's trust, it's truth, it's sacrifice

This story of two mythics matched

From sorrow happiness dispatched

Our lovers prove what most forget

The love you give is the love you get

What You Give

You asked what you could give me
I want to make it clear
You give me what you give no one else
Your loyalty, hopes, and fears

You asked me if I'm happy
And I hope you now can see
That before I knew you, I knew not
Just how happy I could be

You asked if I would hold you
As you bore into my arms
And I promised to protect you
From the malice of false charms

You asked if I could feel
Do you not know I've surrendered?
By the gravity of reality
I was scattered, now I'm centered

Mystery

I gave up trying a long time ago

But the more I tried to know her, the more I didn't know

I had stopped crying a long time ago

But the more I looked into her eyes, the more my tears did show

I gave up my song a long time ago

But the more I thought about her, the more my words did flow

She is to me a mystery, a lovely mystery

Staggered am I by her will, her will to let me be

She is to me reality, all my reality

Saved I am by my faith, my faith that she loves me

Into a Space You Crept

Morning sun couldn't rise
Fire in the eyes, eyes, eyes
I can feel you now
I can feel you now

The engine couldn't turn
Blazing wings burned, burned, burned
I have realized
I have realized

Into a space you have crept
I found you in a hidden space I didn't expect
Should I have let her in?
Once she got inside, I dropped my bags and took the ride

A dance above the sky
Red staircase rise, rise, rise
Set the horses free
Set the horses free

Glass mirror like a cell
Secrets do tell, tell, tell
It's a world reborn
It's a world reborn

Into a space you have crept

I found you in a hidden space I didn't expect

Should I have let her in?

Once she got inside, I dropped my bags and took the ride

More

The more I draw, the more you drain
The more you pause, the more I pain
You make me sear like kindling embers
Your absence cold like sunless winters

The more I push, the more you pull
The more you cut, the more I dull
You make me fierce like prowling wolves
Your presence close, I'm draped in wool

The more I gaze, the more you shy
The more you faze, the more I try
You make my work like mining coal
Your caress converts my straw to gold

The more I drive, the more you stall
The more you think, the more I call
You make me strong like ancient stone
Your essence peace like coming home

Ode to a Phoenix

My love a flame for thee I burn

And from thine ashes, I'll return

Thy flaming wings and ruby eyes

Bring light unto the darkest skies

My love a myth that I believe

Thy mystery have I conceived

Her pure heart pumps volcanic bursts

Thou make the best out of the worst

My love the life for which I'd die

Small sacrifice to let her fly

And from the heavens I would see

A better world because of thee

A Song for You

Just before I rose from bed
A lovely song formed in my head
Lovely words, lovely rhymes
Reflecting on all our good times
I lost that song unto the haze
Consciousness, an endless maze
Now I write, my mind contrite
Of what I left in the twilight

It was a song, a song for you
Inspired by all those good things you do
It was a song, for you and I
And how on you I so rely

Now I'm up, the day wears on
Did you know to you all my thoughts belong?
We sit and talk, this is our time
My comfort this, that you're mine
But I can't help it, I'm remiss
This song, it would have been a hit
Millions would have bought my song
They'd feel true love, it's power strong

It was a song, a song for you
Inspired by all those good things you do
It was a song, for you and I
And how on you I so rely

I leave you this, these scattered thoughts
They are not what my heart had wrought
You inside my mind is gold
My phantom song did so unfold
Though the words be lost in space
My love for you will win the race
For every moment that we make
Becomes a song when I awake

It was a song, a song for you
Inspired by all those good things you do
It was a song, for you and I
And how on you I so rely

I Love Your Crazy

Admittedly a part of me
Feeds off your insanity
Waiting here expectantly
It inspires me, your angry

If I love your calm, then I love your storms
My love for you is a hive that swarms

So let it go and get it out
Run around, scream and shout
And when you're finally out of breath
I'll take you home and grant you rest

Certainly it's plain to see
We cannot go it separately
Treading oh so carefully
Through thorny fields of vanity

If I love your calm, then I love your storms
My love for you is a hive that swarms

Come take my hand and let's go dance
Let's spin the top of our romance
In every way I'll let you be
I love your sane and crazy

Tactfully I'm writing down
These thoughts in which I slowly drown
Eagerly and selfishly
Our ever after happily

Don't Be to Me a Memory

Don't be to me a memory
You are the air that I now breathe
And if you were ever to leave
In love, no longer I'd believe

Don't be to me a memory
You are the proof that I did need
Release me from this binding greed
My heart for your love will concede

Don't be to me a memory
As springtime turns the dead limbs green
My eyes on you the best thing seen
You make me fly; you gave me wings

Don't be to me a memory
You on my side is victory
No more have I uncertainty
Ignited by your energy

Don't be to me a memory
Despite death's sullen, cold decree
This mortal life I give to thee
My soul is yours eternally

Give Me Your Best

Give me your best
I'll give you my all
Give me your best
Make me stand tall

Give me your worst
I'll give you my best
Give me your worst
I'll pass every test

Into me and out of me
Where no one else will see
The parts unknown, the parts unseen
Into depths no one else has been

Give me your best
I'll give you my joy
Give me your best
Let me be your boy

Give me your worst
I'll give you my voice
Give me your worst
You're still my one choice

Into me and out of me

What you see no one else will see

The parts unknown, the parts unseen

Into depths no one else has been

My Phoenix

I see a face I've seen before
Staring at me from youth's door
Unburdened years I do adore
My phoenix could I not love more

I know these years have strung us out
Yet from the shadows we will tout
They will know what we're about
Now the rains dry up this drought

Age we yes and while we're grasping
For another hour gasping
My phoenix has been broadcasting
Life is short, love everlasting

My End

She's my end, my falling skies
My world revolves within her eyes
Joys pour out like infant cries
Through faith true love is realized

She's my end, my dying word
In my last breath her name uttered
Together we shall be interred
A happy heart is one that's earned

She's my end, she's my end
She's my lover in the wind
As our worlds end, ours begins
She's the purpose till my end

She's my end, my burning heart
Can vision's actions not depart?
Passion breaks the waves apart
Fingers praise a brave new start

She's my end, unyielding flame
Sacrifice to her my name
Settle we not for the same
Hearts lost to the sea reclaimed

She's my end, she's my end
She's my lover in the wind
As our worlds end, ours begins
She's the purpose till my end

She's my end, I give her me
My peace is her divinity
Hope the force that keeps men free
These final words are my decree

She's my end, she's my end
She's my lover in the wind
As our worlds end, ours begins
She's the purpose till my end

Mansion

I built a mansion long ago
In a place no travelers go
Hidden well amongst the trees
Far from men and their disease

Halls were long as they were bare
Dining halls, no feasts to share
Bedrooms scattered everywhere
Visitors, my only fear

Often would I walk the grounds
Choruses of birds would sound
Hailing the peace which abounds
In a world with none around

Some seek purpose, wanting more
Loneliness what I adore
Human beings, quite the chore
To them I swore, nevermore

No good thing is meant to last
Distort we all our sullied past
A wandering thought to wind was cast
To grant people one more chance

Glass things, some things, wish to break
Such things delight when the earth quakes
Free will a servant to our fate
I should have built a stronger gate

To make a choice to let one in
You pull a thread, but to what end?
I did not know what would begin
If I invited this one in

Courage mustered, I so chose
I'd open up, to one disclose
Came she to me one spring night
Stagecoach guided by firelight

When she knocked upon my door
I felt something long ignored
Something hidden but held dear
A simple thing, one simple fear

As she passed the entranceway
There were no words for me to say
Speechless I, a rarity
Yet in silence, clarity

Her robes were red, her eyes were hazel
A painting set on golden easel
She did not care that I was weak
She did not care I could not speak

Instead we took to clean my mansion
Dusting off the dank expansion
Cleaning every nook and cranny
Accepting lack of sanity

Before I knew what had begun
I could see two becoming one
No greater proof than this one thing
Together we, effective team

Now my mansion is no longer
A weakness, no, it makes me stronger
Because I let the right one in
Because I know I'm forgiven

Proud

You asked me to write you, so what could I say?

I have written how I love you in oh so many ways

But I knew that you were hungry, and I knew you wanted more

I knew you wanted me to break through all of your locked doors

Here, take these little verses and hide them in your heart

Let me fill your day with gladness, knowing I'll never depart

It is simple to explain this, because you make me so alive

You have become my hope and honor and my full and swelling pride

Proud to be the man at your side

Proud that we no longer must hide

Proud to be the fire in your eyes

Proud to be the shoulder for your cries

Proud to be the one you call

Proud you give me all your all

Proud that we will never fall

Proud that we can both stand tall

Thus, with these little tokens, come cash in and claim your praise

Be the stars that light my evening and the sun that lights my days

For you are my one true lover, and my eyes on you are fixed

That you are my fiery creature, oh you, my love, you're my phoenix

Say It Again

Sitting here and thinking of a new thing I could say
Something that's been said before, but in my own way
Poets and playwrights of old to each their own art play
Songwriters and rockers farm the passion that we graze

It's my turn to say it, so let me say it again
Her love never gets old, and for her it never ends
I can't help but sing it, so let me say it again
Swear to love her the way we do when love begins

Now it is my time to turn a tree into a tale
I hope that my love adores it; let not my words her fail
Let it be to her a force, as snow upon a gale
Make her heart alight on stars, as wind upon a sail

It's my turn to say it, so let me say it again
Her love never gets old, and for her it never ends
I can't help but sing it, so let me say it again
Swear to love her like the way we do when love begins

I don't really care if someone wrote it down before
You make me feel alive, so I'm going to say it more
I don't care if many others write about *amore*
My universe now swarms with the dreams she has restored

It's my turn to say it, so let me say it again

Her love never gets old and for her it never ends

I can't help but sing it, so let me say it again

Swear to love her the way we do when love begins

A Poem for You

You asked me to write a poem
Well what else could I do?
Thy faithful servant shall I be
Craft I this new melody

Many hours my mind has dwelt on you
You make pale eyes turn icy blue
What better way to give thee praise
Than love thee each and every day?

All fields of green have thorny guards
I see it now, though from afar
While pride may prejudice my thought
I know that love is not for naught

You show it well, I hide it well
Sometimes heaven seems like hell
A good thing oft can wander wrong
Let's guide it by this little song

When you need to find your place
When fear gets into your crawl space
Repeat these simple words of truth
You love me, and I love you

In Sickness and in Health

In sickness and in health
It's but a vow, but it's our wealth
For the better or worse
We'll make it through, for we're friends first

As you suffer from the chill
Of the unrelenting cold
Let me be your remedy
Let my warmth in you take hold

With my body, I thee worship
Angelic promise from my lips
To be yours in the mirror
Reflections salve the unknown terror

As I've suffered from the chill
Of the unrelenting cold
You have been my remedy
I feel your warmth in me take hold

In our life and in our death
To our last undying breath
Let us suffer not the wrath
Of living life without our match

The Great Divide

There's a line between the great divide
And soon I'll have to choose a side
One path unknown, one path unclear
One path from which I've never veered

There's a time between the birth and bar
And time now proves I'll not be far
Until the bell tolls, let me be
I choose this serendipity

Life's a million stories, and so few know their role
But I know she is my story, for she's occupied my soul
Life's a million mysteries for those who live by fate
Oh how her charm can disarm, I've met my match, my mate

There's a line between the great divide
Is all my confidence just pride?
The many barbs of risk we bear
Are armored by the joy we share

There's a time between the child and man
Strength and mercy form calloused hands
Her presence is my surety
And she makes me my maturity

Life's a million stories and so few do know their role
But I know she is my story, for she's occupied my soul
Life's a million mysteries, for those who live by fate
And how her charm can so disarm, I've met my match, my mate

Mutiny

You called me out into the night
Promised to make it all right
I'd been alone so many years
Wrestling with these hopes and fears

You didn't make the choices hard
This rendezvous beneath the stars
After time alone with you
A storm on the horizon looms

Inside of me came mutiny
A raging sea's ferocity
A volcano's calamity
A victim's darkest memory

I hope you feel the love you've made
It will stay with me until my grave
Come, take my hand and beating heart
We'll never have to be apart

You are to me a ruby gem
The precious stone of a best friend
I'll value you and all you are
And catch a burning, falling star

Inside of me felt destiny

A prophet's serendipity

A painter's stroke of brilliancy

A sinner's act of charity

Clarity

She gave me the gift of clarity

Hence came this song from charity

In me, so much disparity

She is the world's true rarity

She takes away uncertainty

Lets me live in her rent-free

Protected by her purity

Her promise, my security

Like rain on drought-filled forest trees

She is all my prosperity

Take my heart, take all of me

Surrender I this property

Time Set Aside

Hello, my love, I must confide
For you, my love, time set aside
I know you love my little rhymes
You love them each and every time

So, my love, here comes another
For you, my love, it is no bother
I know your smile beams bright and wide
When for, my love, time set aside

Sweet, my love, my love is so sweet
You swept this man right off his feet
Oh look at how his new heart beats
For nothing else my time competes

Pray, my love, we never need pray
Pray, my love, for less onerous days
Our love persists in space and time
Quantum phantoms always will shine

Do you, my love, enjoy this work?
Do you, my love, see what you've unearthed?
Don't fear, my love, as storms may swell
My holes, my love, you fill them well

Goodbye, my love, just for a while

You know, my love, I've made you smile

I know you love my little rhymes

You love them each and every time

She Took My Pen

She took my pen from me
She made it sing a new song
She showed me a new path
She taught me how to dance

She strolled into my dreams
She grabbed my weathered hands
She straightened all my ways
She covered all my sins

She, how she makes me smile
She, how I trust her like a child
She, how she understands
She, how she shifts the sands

She stole from me my fears
She hid them far from me
She flew us into space
She lit up the universe

She purposed me to feel
She revealed the inner truths
She fashioned us a life
She crafted the device

She, how she makes me smile

She, how I trust her like a child

She, how she understands

She, how she shifts the sands

Lover

She finds a way to pass the time
These hours I thought were mine
But now my days are lost to sky
Oh love, thou art divine

Lover of my soul
Lover of my mind
Lover of the little parts the world will leave behind
Lover take my hand
Lover take my heart
Lover take my life before this world I must depart

Her many forms like falling snow
Facades they be, her spirit gold
But now I see she is aflame
Oh love, an endless show

Lover of my soul
Lover of my mind
Lover of the little parts the world will leave behind
Lover take my hand
Lover take my heart
Lover take my life before this world I must depart

She finds a way to make amends

From fire and ice, she both defends

But showed me she with veil down

Oh love, thou art my friend

Lover of my soul

Lover of my mind

Lover of the little parts the world will leave behind

Lover take my hand

Lover take my heart

Lover take my life before this world I must depart

Made in United States
Orlando, FL
21 October 2023